GOOD MORNING,
I LOVE YOU,

GOOD MORNING,
I LOVE YOU,
Violet!

For Jackson, Luke, Caroline, and Lawson

–Shauna Shapiro

For my wonderful daughter, Heidi

–Susi Schaefer

Sounds True
Boulder, CO 80306

Text © 2023 Shauna Shapiro and Jennifer Adams
Illustrations © 2023 Susi Schaefer

Published 2023

Book design by Meredith Jarrett

Printed in China

Library of Congress Cataloging-in-Publication Data

Names: Shapiro, Shauna L., author. | Schaefer, Susi, illustrator.
Title: Good morning, I love you, Violet! / by Shauna Shapiro;
    illustrated by Susi Schaefer.
Description: Boulder, CO : Sounds True, 2023.
Identifiers: LCCN 2022055270 (print) | LCCN 2022055271 (ebook) |
    ISBN 9781649630315 (hardcover) | ISBN 9781649630322 (ebook)
Subjects: CYAC: Self-esteem--Fiction. | LCGFT: Picture books.
Classification: LCC PZ7.1.S48343 Go 2023 (print) | LCC PZ7.1.S48343
    (ebook) | DDC [E]–dc23
LC record available at https://lccn.loc.gov/2022055270
LC ebook record available at https://lccn.loc.gov/2022055271

10 9 8 7 6 5 4 3 2 1

GOOD MORNING,
I LOVE YOU,
Violet!

By SHAUNA SHAPIRO
Illustrated by
SUSI SCHAEFER

sounds true
BOULDER, COLORADO

On Monday,

Violet didn't want to get up.

She pulled the covers over her head.

"Good morning, Violet," her mom called from the kitchen.

But it didn't seem like a good morning at all.

The air outside Violet's blankets felt chilly, and it was still dark. At breakfast, her cereal was wet and soggy.

At school, Violet forgot the answer to #6 on her quiz.

"I can never remember things," she thought.

At lunch, Violet spilled juice on her sweater.

"I'm so clumsy!" she cried.

At recess, she missed blocking a goal at soccer.

"I'm just not good at sports," she told herself.

Violet's class had a special visitor that afternoon. Dr. Freedman was a scientist.

"Sometimes we talk unkindly to ourselves," she told them, "and that hurts our happiness."

"I'm going to teach you a practice of planting seeds of kindness," she said. "It seems simple, but it's powerful and can change the way you feel."

"Every day when you wake up, put your hand on your heart, take a breath, and say to yourself,

'Good morning, I love you.'"

"Planting seeds of kindness sounds nice," said Lila.

"My dad told me about that," said Xavier, looking up from his book.

"What you practice grows stronger."

"That's right," said Dr. Freedman. "By planting seeds of kindness, you can grow happiness."

"**I'll try it!**" said Jackson.

Violet wasn't sure. It sounded silly to her. How would saying she loved herself change anything?

On Tuesday, Violet woke up and remembered she was supposed to tell herself,

"Good morning, I love you."

"I don't think so," Violet muttered.

That morning at recess, Violet's friends gathered around.

"Did you try it?" Jackson asked. "Did you say, 'Good morning, I love you'?"

"I did," Lila smiled shyly. "It was kind of nice. Planting seeds of kindness."

"I did too," Jackson said.

"What you practice grows stronger," Xavier said.

Violet looked away.

On Wednesday morning, Violet heard her mom call from the kitchen.

"Good morning, Violet. I made waffles."

Violet thought about telling herself, "Good morning, I love you," but it felt awkward.

"I'm not saying it!" she said.

In the kitchen, Mom gave Violet a big hug.

"Waffles mean 'I love you!'"

Mom said. "I love you, Violet."

That was a nice way to start the day,
Violet thought: **with love.**

At school Jackson said, "It's weird, but I really like telling myself,

'Good morning, I love you.'"

"It makes me feel warm and happy inside," said Lila.

"What you practice grows stronger," said Xavier.

"Did you try it yet, Violet?" Jackson asked.

Violet gritted her teeth. "How would it help?" she asked.

"**You're planting seeds of kindness,**" Lila said.

"It's easy," Jackson said.

Violet remembered how good it felt when her mom told her she loved her. And she trusted her friends. "Okay," she said. "I'll try."

On Thursday morning, Violet's blanket felt cozy. Her mom said, "Good morning, I love you, Violet."

Violet remembered promising her friends that she would try planting seeds of kindness. "I can do this," she said to herself.

She put her hand on her heart, took a deep breath, and said,

"Good morning, I love you, Violet."

Violet waited for something to happen. She felt a tiny bit of warmth in her heart. Was that what her friends were talking about?

On Friday morning, Violet woke up looking forward to school. Friday was her favorite day of the week. Before she got out of bed, Violet put her hand on her heart, took a breath, and said,

"Good morning, I love you, Violet."

This time she felt warmth in her heart for sure!

In art class, Violet spilled her watercolors.

"Don't worry," Violet told her teacher.

"I'm good at cleaning up messes."

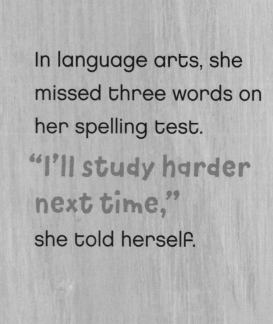

In language arts, she missed three words on her spelling test.

"I'll study harder next time," she told herself.

At recess, Jackson made two soccer goals and Violet didn't make any.

"Good job, Jackson," Violet told him.

"I like having you on our team," Jackson said.

Soon it was time to pack her backpack and go home.

"Have a good weekend," Lila called.

"See you on Monday," Jackson said.

"Later," Xavier said.

"Remember to practice planting seeds of kindness," Violet's friends called after her.

SCHOOL

"I will," Violet promised.

On Saturday morning, Violet slept until the sun woke her.

Everyone in Violet's house was sleeping in, too.

Violet smiled at the warmth of the sun.

Then she put her hand on her heart and whispered,

"Good morning, I love you, Violet."

A Note from the Author for Parents and Teachers

I believe self-love is a superpower. When we treat ourselves with kindness, it turns on the learning centers of the brain and gives us the resources to face challenges and learn from our mistakes. Transformation requires a compassionate mindset, not shame.

And yet, people often worry that self-love will make them lazy, self-indulgent, or self-absorbed. Science shows just the opposite: people with greater self-love are more compassionate toward others, more successful and productive, and more resilient to stress.

The best news of all: self-love can be learned. We can rewire the structure of our brain and strengthen the neural circuitry of love toward ourselves and others. Each time we practice self-love, we grow this pathway.

Good Morning, I Love You, Violet! offers a road map for strengthening your child's brain circuitry of deep calm, contentment, and self-love. It is built on principles of psychology and neuroscience and offers a simple yet powerful practice.

As a mother, when asked what I believe is the most important thing we can teach our children, I always answer "self-love." Learning to be on our own team and to treat ourselves with kindness is life-changing. There is no greater gift we can give our children. There is no greater gift we can give ourselves.

May this book plant seeds of kindness that ripple out into the world.

—Shauna Shapiro, PhD